The Little Fox's Adventures

Text: Ulf Stark • Illustrations: Petra Svanbäck

Everyone in the forest loves the little fox. She's so sweet! But she's always running around. She goes rushing into the bushes and screams, scaring all the birds away.

"Can't you be quiet?" the others ask her.

"Yes I can – if I want to," says the fox. "Because I can do ANYTHING."

So she keeps quiet for a while and creeps around instead. Creeping around is another thing she likes doing. She creeps around the animals' legs until the moose trips and bangs his head on a tree!

"Ah, Ah, Ah, ACHOO!" sneezes the moose, because he has snow on his nose. "Can't you stop creeping around like that?"

"Yes I can – if I want to," says the fox. "Because I can do ANYTHING."

5

She has stopped creeping around now. Instead she grabs the wolf's tail with her teeth and lets the wolf pull her along in the snow. Wheeeee, that is great fun! Until the wolf stops.

"What do you think you are doing?!" he roars. "Can't you keep still and quiet, just for fifteen minutes?"

"Yes I can – if I want to," says the fox. "Because I can do ANYTHING."

Now the fox is lying still outside her den. She is listening to the wind whistling through the trees, and she's watching the snow.
"I can, I can, I can keep still and quiet," she thinks.
   Suddenly, she sees a bright red ball between the trees.
   "I want that ball," she thinks. "And I can do anything I like."

She jumps over rocks. She slides down the snowy hills. And she thinks: "Wow, what fun I'm going to have with that red ball! I'm going to push it up in the air with my nose!"

And off she runs.

But suddenly the red ball is gone. It gets darker and darker. And cold too, brrr! The fox runs one way. Then she runs a different way. She wants to get home to her nice warm den.

But there is something she *can't* do. She can't find her way home.

13

Soon the moon and stars come out. The little fox is tired. She is alone and afraid. And cold too.

"Ooweee!" she howls. "Oh why did my legs run off with me?"

All of a sudden, a sleepy head pops out from under a pile of snow and old leaves. It's the snake.

"Stop howling!" hisses the snake. "You woke me up."

"I'm sorry," whimpers the fox. "I am lost and very cold. Are you going to eat me up?"

"Of course I'm not!" yawns the snake. "Come on into my lair and I'll warm you up."

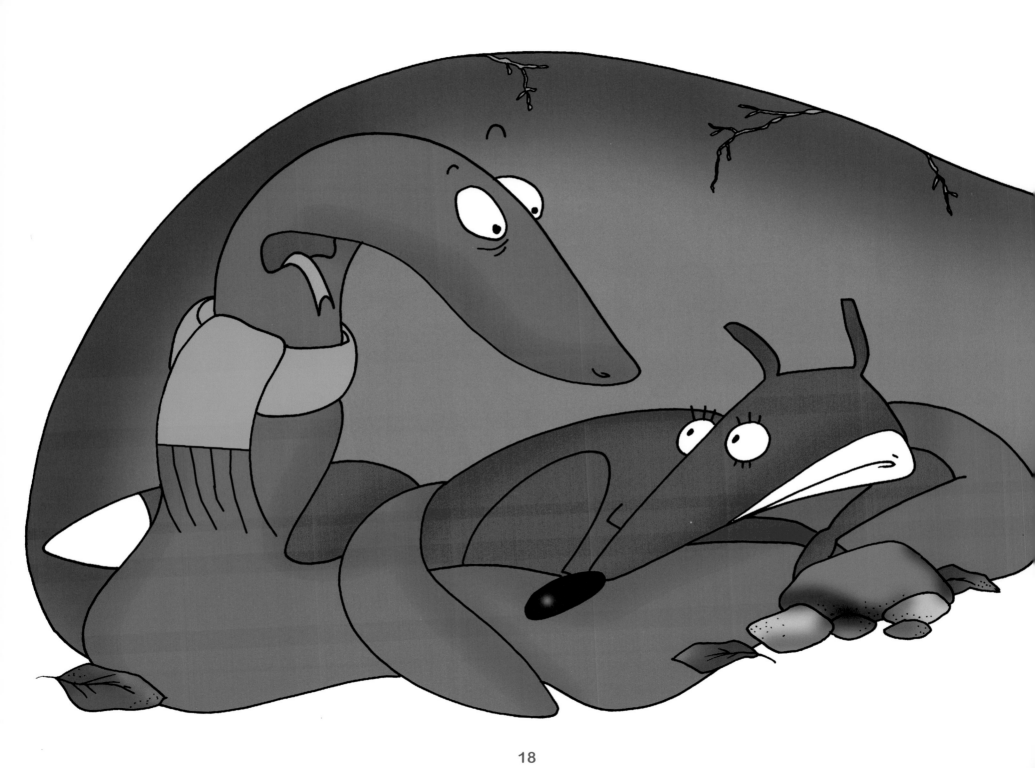

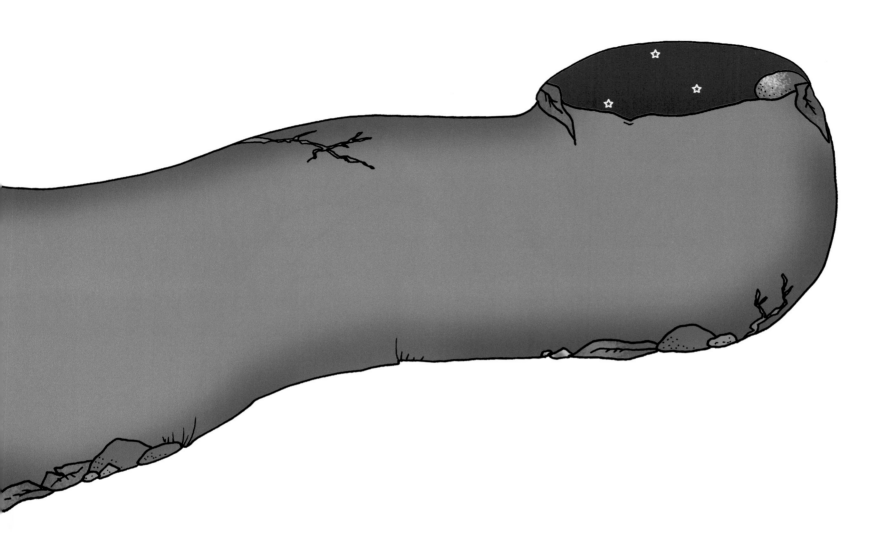

"By the way, how did you get lost?" wonders the snake.

"I saw a red ball," says the fox. "Then all of a sudden it was gone. And then it got dark."

"And I thought foxes were supposed to be smart," says the snake. "That was the sun going down. Lie down and rest and I'll keep you warm."

20

Now the wolf and the moose have discovered that the fox is missing.
They look behind rocks, and under bushes. They look everywhere.
   "Where can she be?" says the wolf.
   "Yes, where has she gone?" says the moose.
They continue looking deeper and deeper into the forest.

When the sun comes up, the moose is leaning against a tree. The wolf is lying on the ground. They have been looking for the fox all night.

"I think she's gone forever," sighs the wolf. "And she was so sweet."

"And so full of energy," says the moose. "I remember her running around and around my legs."

"Yes, and she bit my tail," says the wolf. "Oh I wish she was doing it again now."

Suddenly they hear a faint cough. The wolf stands up and sniffs around in the air.

"This way!" he calls after a while. "It smells of fox this way!"

He rushes to a mound and scratches away at it, sending snow and leaves into the air. And there she is, the little fox. All wrapped up in the snake.

"Oh there you are, dear little fox!" howls the wolf.

"The snake hasn't been horrible, has he?" asks the moose.

"I just gave her somewhere to sleep," says the snake. "Here in my house. Well… it *used* to be a house. Thanks a lot for stopping by!"

Once they have given the little fox a hug, thanked the snake, said sorry for breaking his house and helped him build it again, the animals set off back to their own part of the forest.

The snake has given the fox his green scarf because she has caught a bit of a cold.

She is riding on the back of the wolf and waving with the scarf.

"Bye bye snake!" she calls.

"Oh we are *so* happy we found you!" say the wolf and the moose when they return. "But how could you just run off like that?"

"I can do ANYTHING," says the fox. "Or well, nearly anything," she adds after a while. "Tomorrow I am going to pull your tail."

"I'm going to pull yours today," says the moose.

And he does. The fox laughs. It's music to their ears.

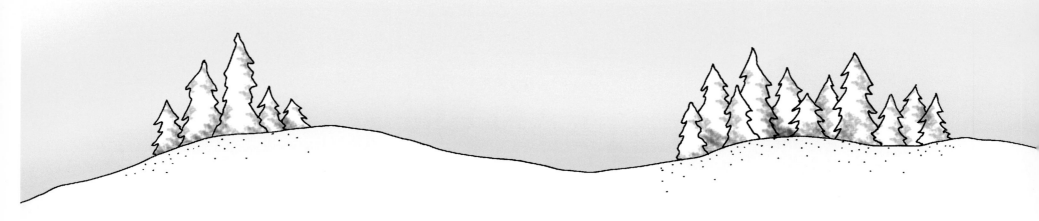

THE END

© BARNSLIG
The Little Fox's Adventures
Project manager: Lena Allblom, IKEA FAMILY
Project co-ordinator: Anders Truedsson, TITEL Books AB
Fact checker: Fredrik Bengtsson, Children's IKEA Range Communicator
Text: Ulf Stark
Illustrations: Petra Svanbäck
Graphic design: Pierre Österholm
Typesetting: Gyllene Snittet
International editor and IKEA verbal identity adviser: Janet Colletti, Boco Text Studio/Boco AB
North American adaptation: Boco Text Studio/Boco AB
Translation: Comactiva Translations AB
Produced by IKEA FAMILY
Paper: Symbol Freelife Satin FCS
Printing: Litopat S.p.A, Italy 2010